P9-DVU-987

PANCAKES

FOR

BREAKFAST

WITHDRAWN

PANCAKES FOR BREAKFAST

BY

TOMIE dePAOLA

HARCOURT, INC.

Orlando   Austin   New York   San Diego   Toronto   London

FOR BETTY CAVE ♡

Copyright © 1978 by Tomie dePaola

All rights reserved. No part of this publication may be reproduced or transmitted
in any form or by any means, electronic or mechanical, including photocopy, recording,
or any information storage and retrieval system, without permission in writing from the publisher.

For information about permission to reproduce selections from this book, write to
trade.permissions@hmhco.com or to Permissions, Houghton Mifflin Harcourt
Publishing Company, 3 Park Avenue, 19th Floor, New York, New York 10016.

www.hmhco.com

Voyager Books is a registered trademark of Harcourt, Inc.

LIBRARY OF CONGRESS CATALOGING-IN-PUBLICATION DATA
dePaola, Thomas Anthony.
Pancakes for breakfast.
Summary: A little old lady's attempts to have
pancakes for breakfast are hindered by a scarcity
of supplies and participation of her pets.
[1. Stories without words.]   I. Title.
PZ7.D439PAN   77-15523
ISBN-13: 978-0-15-259455-8   ISBN-l0: 0-15-259455-8
ISBN-13: 978-0-15-670768-8 pb ISBN-l0: 0-15-670768-3 pb

SCP 55 54
4500737959

Manufactured in China

31901064284633